Happy 8th Birthday
Lots of Love
Anthony, Kelly & Lee

Enid Blyton's

TALES FROM TOYLAND

A TEMPLAR BOOK

Produced by The Templar Company plc,
Pippbrook Mill, London Road, Dorking, Surrey RH4 1JE.

This edition produced in the UK for Bookmart Ltd.
Direct sales rights only for the U.K. held by INDEX.
First published in Canada in 1994 by Smithbooks.

This book contains material first published as
They Ran Away Together by Brockhampton, 1948,
The Little Walking House in My First Enid Blyton Book by Latimer House, 1952,
and *The Very Old Teddy Bear* from Enid Blyton's Pennant Series by Macmillan, 1950.

Illustrated by Phil Garner, Mike Dodd and John Bennett
Cover illustration by Mike Dodd

Printed and bound in Singapore

ISBN 1-898784-04-3

Enid Blyton's
TALES FROM TOYLAND

TEMPLAR

CONTENTS

The Toys' Great Adventure

Journey to Rainbow's End

The Very Old Teddy Bear

The Toys' Great Adventure

Peter and Jane were turning out their toy cupboard. It was nearly Christmas time, and they knew they would soon have plenty of new toys.

"We simply must make room for them," said Jane. "We must throw out any toy we don't want. What about this car, Peter?"

"It was very nice when it was new," he said. "But it won't run now because of its bent wheel."

"Then we'll throw it away," said Jane, and she put it into the waste-paper basket.

"Oh look – here's the little rag doll," said Jane, suddenly. "I haven't played with her for ages. Her black hair is very untidy – it looks like a mop!"

So into the basket went Mopsy the rag doll. She fell beside the toy car.

"I used to love this clockwork man," said Peter. "But we lost his key ages ago, so he can't walk now." So into the basket went Mr. Click, the clockwork man.

"Any more to throw away?" said Jane.

"What about this tiny bear?" said Peter, holding him up. "We called him Biggy the Bear because he was so small. Do you remember?"

"Yes," said Jane, taking the little bear. "It's a shame, but he's very dirty, and he's lost an eye."

So Biggy went into the waste-paper basket too!

"There!" said Jane, looking into the empty toy cupboard. "That's everything. Let's clean the shelves and put back the things we are keeping. We'll have a whole shelf empty for our new toys."

They worked hard till bedtime. Their mother was very pleased when she came to take them to bed.

"Well done!" she said. "I'll take this rubbish down to the kitchen. We can put it in the dustbin tomorrow."

Mother took the basket of old toys down to the kitchen and then went off to see the children into bed. The kitchen cat sniffed in the basket to see if there was anything to eat there. But there wasn't.

"Just a lot of dirty old toys," said the cat to herself, as she curled up on the kitchen chair.

After everyone had
gone to bed that night,
everything was dark and quiet
in the kitchen. Not a sound
was to be heard except for the
gentle snoring of the tabby cat.
Suddenly the cat pricked up her
ears. She had heard something.
Was it a mouse? No, the noise was coming
from the waste-paper basket! Mopsy, Mr. Click
and Biggy Bear slowly sat up and peeped over the edge
of the waste-paper basket. The moonlight shone on
them from the kitchen window and they looked at one
another dolefully.

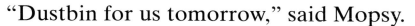

"Dustbin for us tomorrow," said Mopsy.

"Don't you believe it!" said Mr. Click. "I'm not staying here to be popped into the dustbin!"

"But you can't go far without being wound up," said Mopsy. Mr. Click looked very gloomy.

"Yes, you're right. I can walk a few steps and then I come to a stop. What a pity! It would have been fun to run away, and take you and Biggy Bear with me, Mopsy."

"Sh! Here comes the cat!" said Mopsy, and they all slid down into the basket again. Mopsy fell next to the toy car. Suddenly she had an idea.

"Mr. Click!" she whispered. "Do you think the key to the clockwork car would fit you? Shall I try?"

"If you like," said Mr. Click. "But Jane and Peter tried hundreds of other keys and not one worked."

The toys waited until the cat had gone back to sleep. Then Mopsy tried the car key.

"It fits!" said Biggy, excited.

"But it won't turn to wind me up – you just see!" said Mr. Click, gloomily.

"Mr. Click! It *does* turn!" cried Mopsy. "You can walk again."

"Well, what a lovely surprise!" said Mr. Click, smiling. "Mopsy – Biggy – will you come with me? We'll run away and find a dear little house somewhere. We *won't* go into the dustbin!"

"Yes. We'd love to come," said Mopsy and Biggy.

"Wait," said Mr. Click. "My key's dropped out. It's fallen to the bottom of the basket. I shall lose it!"

Mopsy scrabbled about in the basket and found the key. "I shall tie the key to the strings of my apron," she said. "Now we can't possibly lose it!"

"Let's go now!" said Biggy, jigging up and down.

"Wait," said Mr. Click suddenly. "I've had an idea!"

"What is it?" said Biggy Bear and Mopsy.

"Let's take the old toy car with us," said Mr. Click. "We could go for miles in that."

They pulled the car out of the basket on to the kitchen floor. "See – the wheel is bent, but I can easily straighten that," said Mr. Click.

Soon the wheel was quite straight again, and the car could run along well, though it was a bit wobbly. Then Mr. Click straightened the squashed-in roof.

"There!" he said. "It's mended! I'll drive. I used to drive this car round the nursery before it was broken. Get in beside me, Biggy. You get in the back, Mopsy."

The others got in, feeling very excited. Then Mopsy thought of something. "How can we get out of the house? The door is locked."

"Oh, I've thought of that," said Mr. Click. "We'll just drive out of the cat's door!"

And that is what they did! With a clickety-click out they went through the cat's little door. They were out in the garden now. The little car was wobbly, and Biggy and Mopsy clutched the sides hard as they rattled over stones in the gravel path.

The car came to a stop at the end of the garden. Mopsy took the key off her apron string and gave it to Mr. Click to wind up the car again. Then she tied it safely on to her apron string once more.

"We must find somewhere to live," said Mopsy to Mr. Click. "I'm a very good cook. I can look after you both very well indeed."

"Yes, do let's find somewhere," said Biggy Bear. "Somewhere with a tiny garden. I'm such a good gardener, you know. I love digging."

"Right," said Mr. Click. "We'll find a nice little house with a tiny garden for Biggy to dig in. I'd rather like a garage for the car, too. I can look after that. I'm good with cars."

But it wasn't easy to find a house. They looked and looked, but there didn't seem to be any about at all.

"I'm so sleepy," said Mopsy at last. "Can we sleep in the car tonight and look for a house in the morning?"

So Mr. Click parked the car under a hedge and they all fell fast asleep. In the morning, a robin woke them up by singing loudly in their ears.

"Hello, robin!" said Mopsy. "You don't know where we could find a little house with a tiny garden and a garage, do you?"

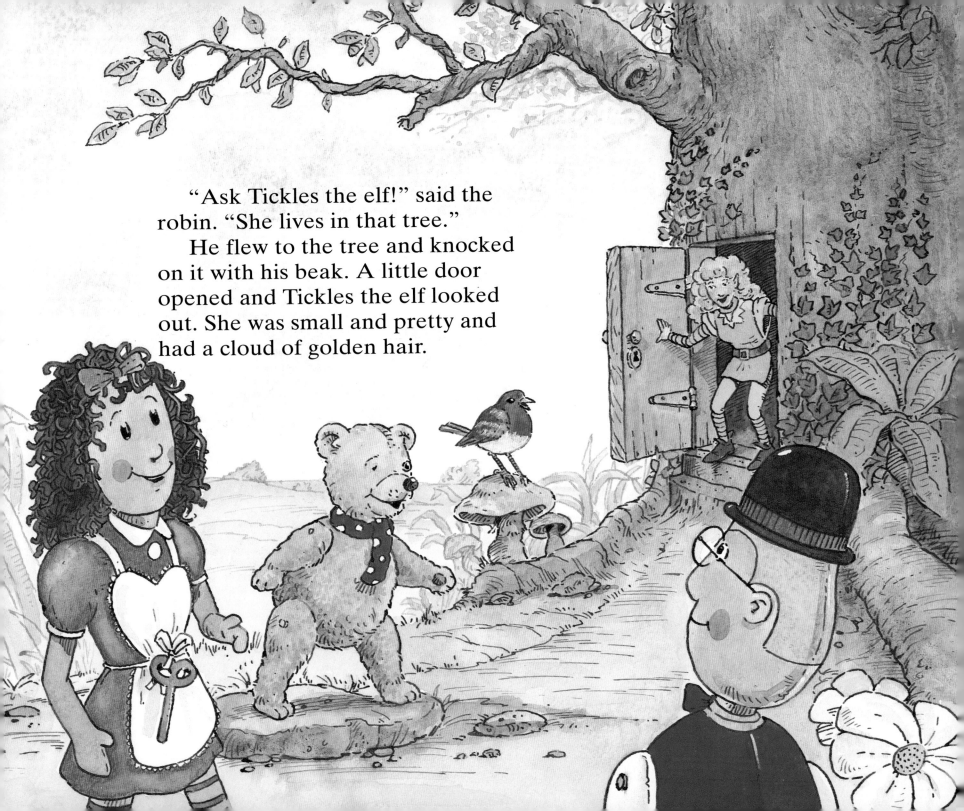

"Ask Tickles the elf!" said the robin. "She lives in that tree."

He flew to the tree and knocked on it with his beak. A little door opened and Tickles the elf looked out. She was small and pretty and had a cloud of golden hair.

"What is it you want?" she said. "A house? Oh yes, I know where there is one to let. Come in and have breakfast with me, then I'll show you the house."

So they all went into Tickles' little round room inside the tree and had a delicious breakfast.

"Now come with me and I'll show you the house !" said Tickles. "You'll love it!"

The house was a very large toadstool with a small door in the stalk. Inside a winding staircase led up to a big room at the top of the toadstool. There were three windows in the roof, so the room was full of light.

"It's lovely!" said Mopsy in delight. "And it's furnished too. What dear little chairs and tables!"

"Is there a garage for the car?" asked Mr. Click.

"Is there a teeny-weeny garden?" asked Biggy.

"No," said Tickles. "It's just a house."

"Well, we'll take it and move in," said Mopsy, sitting down in the chairs to see if they were comfortable.

"Listen!" said Tickles, suddenly. "Oh dear! Whatever shall we do? He's back again!"

"Who's back?"
said Mopsy, Mr. Click
and Biggy Bear.

"The old black horse who lives
in this field," said Tickles. "He's been
away for ages. He's got great big feet.
Once he even knocked down a toadstool house."

"Quick! Get out!" shouted Mr. Click, as the
heavy footsteps came nearer and nearer.

Clip-clop, clip-clop! Hrrrrrrrumph! Tickles and the others almost fell down the stairs in their hurry. They reached the safety of Tickles' tree just in time, watching in horror as one of the horse's shaggy hooves knocked down the dear little toadstool house. Mopsy and Tickles screamed.

"It's broken! It's ruined!" cried Tickles. The top had broken off the stalk, and tiny chairs lay on the grass. Mopsy began to cry.

"Never mind. It didn't have a garage," said Mr. Click, trying to comfort her.

"And there wasn't even a teeny-weeny garden," said Biggy Bear.

"I don't mind about those," sobbed Mopsy. "It was the house I wanted. Now we'll have to find another."

"Well, wind me up, and we'll go off in the car again," said Mr. Click. "Cheer up, Mopsy. I'll find a beautiful house soon."

They said goodbye to poor Tickles, climbed into the car, and drove off. They all felt very sad. It had been such a dear little house. Would they ever find another?

They drove about all that day and the next. They had meals with all sorts of people, who were very kind to them. A family of rabbits gave them a salad supper. A little green goblin shared his breakfast with them. Two pixies took them into their home under the hedge

and gave them dinner. But they didn't find a house.

Then, that afternoon, they came to a garden. There was a big house there, rather like the one that Jane and Peter lived in, with a wide verandah. Mr. Click drove the little car on to the verandah to get out of the rain. In the corner was a big box of toy bricks! It was partly covered by a dirty old cloth. Dust and cobwebs lay on both box and cloth.

"Look! These bricks must have been forgotten!" said Mr. Click. "No one has used them for ages. Let's build a house with them!"

"What a lovely idea!" said Mopsy. "Do you know how to build a house, Mr. Click?"

"I think so," he replied. "Biggy can help me. We'll build a house in the corner here. We can build a garage, too."

"What about a garden?" asked Biggy.

"Oh, you and your garden!" said Mr. Click. "You can't *build* gardens, Biggy. You have to make them. Come and help me to carry these bricks."

Mr. Click was very busy as they built the house. He ran about here and there, and Mopsy had to wind him up dozens of times. Two windows went in, a back door and a front door, and steps up to the front. And then, the roof went on! There were three chimneys so they each put one on. Then they opened the front door and walked inside their new house.

"It's lovely," said Mopsy, happily. "We shall have to buy some furniture, but we can sleep on the floor till we have beds."

"I'm so tired I could sleep anywhere," said Biggy Bear yawning.

Next morning, they left the house, shutting the front door behind them, and went to find some breakfast. A little mouse they met kindly gave them some cheese and a bit of pie. People were really very kind to them. They told him about their new house.

"Come and see it," said Mopsy. So they took the little mouse to the verandah. But, oh dear, what a dreadful shock they had when they got there!

The house wasn't there any longer! All the bricks were packed away neatly in the box once more.

"So they did belong to somebody," said Mopsy sadly. "And the Somebody has come along and unbuilt our house, and packed it all away. It's no good building it again. We'll have to find another!"

"I know where there's a house!" said the little mouse, suddenly. "It might just do for you nicely. But it's only got one room – though it's a very big one!"

He led them down the garden, with Mr. Click bumping along in the car behind him. They came to a small wooden building, with a very large open doorway.

"It's a funny place," said Mopsy, peering inside. "A doorway and no door to shut! And not a single window to let in light and air! I don't think I like it very much."

"Why is there all this straw on the floor?" said Biggy Bear. "It's very prickly."

"There's no garage," said Mr. Click. "But this one room is so large that the car could live here with us."

"There's no garden, either," said Biggy.

"You could perhaps dig a bit of the ground outside the house for a garden," said the little mouse.

"Yes. I suppose I could," said Biggy. "Who does the house belong to, mouse?"

"I don't know who it belongs to," said the mouse. "I've only just come to this place myself. I should move in if I were you, before anyone else does."

"Right," said Mr. Click. "Help me in with the car, please Biggy."

They were all very tired when they had dragged the car inside. They sat down to get their breath. Mopsy leaned against Mr. Click, and Biggy leaned against the car. In a few minutes they were all asleep!

Suddenly a great big head looked into the doorway and big panting breaths filled the air. Mopsy screamed.

"What's all this?" said a deep, wuffy voice. "Who are you? What are you doing in my kennel?"

There was a long silence. A kennel! So that's what the wooden house was. No wonder it had no door and no windows. It belonged to a dog.

"We must go," said Mr. Click, in a small voice. "Sorry, Mr. Dog! We came in here not knowing it belonged to you. We'll go!"

And very sadly Mr. Click, Mopsy and Biggy Bear dragged out the car, wound it up, got into it and set off.

"We must try and find another house," said poor Mopsy. "How unlucky we are!"

The car chugged on for a long, long way. It stopped by a signpost. Mopsy leaned out to read it.

"To Pixie-Land," she read. "Well, we might as well go there. There might be an empty house there."

So on they went. They knew they were in Pixie-Land because of all the little folk they met. But they couldn't find a house even there! There was only an empty rabbit-hole to let, and they had to take that. It was very sad because it wasn't a house, there was no garage, and, of course, not even a garden.

Not far off was a beautiful house, big and full of lovely furniture, with a garage full of cars, and a perfectly lovely garden. And it was empty!

"It belongs to Princess Starlight," said Mopsy. "She is away ill. It's such a shame. All the furniture is getting dusty, and the cars need cleaning and the garden is a mass of weeds."

"Perhaps we could clean everything up a little," said Mr. Click. "I'd love to polish those cars."

So, when their work was finished each day, the three friends climbed over the wall of the Princess's house and went to work there. Biggy was so happy digging and weeding. He sang in a little growly voice all the time. Mopsy climbed in through the kitchen window. She found mops and brooms and dusters and started to clean the house.

"If I can't have a house of my own to clean, I'll clean somebody else's," she thought.

As for Mr. Click, he was so happy that he whistled loudly as he washed and polished each car.

They were very happy in their secret work.

"The house looks beautiful inside!" said Mopsy.

"The garden is spick and span and full of flowers!" said Biggy Bear, who looked dirtier than ever.

"The cars shine as if they were new," said Mr. Click.

And then something happened! One day when they went to the house they found the gates and the front door open, and all the windows were thrown open too! They stood and stared.

"Her Highness the Princess Starlight is expected back today," said the postman, going in with a lot of letters. "Somebody is getting the place ready for her."

"No more cleaning up that lovely house!" said Mopsy, sadly.

"No more digging in the garden," said Biggy.

"No more looking after those beautiful cars," said Mr. Click. "Come on – we'd better go home."

"I do hope the Princess won't mind that we've been in her house and garden," said Mopsy, alarmed. "I don't think anyone ever saw us. But you never know!"

The next day there was a big notice up on the walls of the nearby village.

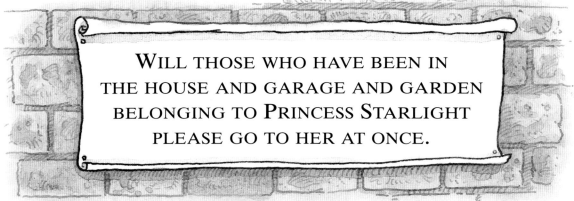

WILL THOSE WHO HAVE BEEN IN
THE HOUSE AND GARAGE AND GARDEN
BELONGING TO PRINCESS STARLIGHT
PLEASE GO TO HER AT ONCE.

"Will she punish us?" said Mopsy, looking frightened.

"Don't let's go," said Biggy.

"We *must* go," said Mr. Click. "We can't be cowards. I expect all that will happen will be that we'll be sent away in disgrace."

They went to see the Princess Starlight. She was very lovely. They bowed low before her.

"We're the ones who came and trespassed," said Mr. Click, humbly. "You see, Your Highness, we so

badly wanted a house with a garden and garage for ourselves, but we couldn't find one, so we sort of borrowed yours. But we didn't live here."

"And we didn't do any harm," said Biggy. "We just looked after everything."

"And I didn't break anything, honestly," said Mopsy. "I do hope you won't punish us too much."

The Princess looked at the little clockwork man with his smily face, at little black-haired Mopsy, and the dirty one-eyed bear. She smiled sweetly.

"I hope you won't find your punishment too hard," she said. "I am going to make you come and live here! Mopsy, you are to be my housekeeper. Biggy, you shall be my head gardener. Mr. Click, you are to be my chauffeur, and drive me anywhere I want to go."

"Oh!" said Mopsy. "OH! That's no punishment. It's wonderful! I don't know what to say!"

"And as soon as I can, I shall have a little house built especially for you," said the Princess. "Can you move in today? I was so pleased to find the house and the garden and the cars looking so lovely when I came home! Thank you all so much."

Well, Mr. Click, Mopsy and Biggy moved in that very day. Biggy had a bath and came out clean. The Princess gave him a new eye and he looked really handsome. Then the Princess combed Mopsy's hair and tied it in two bunches. She looked very pretty.

That's a year ago now. The Princess kept her word and built them a tiny house with a tiny garden and a tiny garage for the old clockwork car. They are all very happy indeed, and Biggy grows bigger cabbages than any other gardener there!

"This is better than going into the dustbin!" Mopsy often says. "Whatever would Peter and Jane say if they could see us now?"

They *would* be surprised, wouldn't they?

Journey to Rainbow's End

If it hadn't been for Pincher, the puppy, the adventure would never have happened. Jill and Simon were taking him for a walk in Cuckoo Wood, and he was mad with joy. He tore here, there and everywhere, barking and jumping for all he was worth.

The children laughed at him, especially when he tumbled head over heels and rolled over and over on the grass. He was such a fat, roly-poly puppy, and they loved him very much.

Then something happened. Pincher dived under a bramble bush, and came out with something in his mouth. It was a string of small sausages!

"Now wherever could he have got those from?" said Jill, in surprise. She soon knew, for out from under the bush ran a little fellow dressed in red and yellow, with a pointed cap on his head. He wasn't much taller than the puppy, but he had a very big voice.

"You bad dog!" he shouted. "You've stolen the sausages I bought for dinner! Bring them back at once or I'll turn you into a mouse!"

Pincher took no notice. He galloped about with the sausages, enjoying himself very much. Then he sat down to eat them! That was too much for the small man. He rushed at Pincher and struck him on the nose with a tiny silver stick. At the same time he shouted out a string of queer words, so strange that Jill and Simon felt quite frightened. They knew they were magic words, although they had never heard any before.

And then, before their eyes, Pincher began to grow small! He grew smaller and smaller and smaller, and at last he was as tiny as a mouse. In fact, he *was* a mouse, though he didn't know it! He couldn't think what had happened to him. He scampered up to Jill and Simon, barking in a funny little mouse-like squeak.

The children were dreadfully upset. They picked up the tiny mouse and stroked him. Then they looked for the little man to ask him if he would please change Pincher back to a dog again.

But he had gone. Not a sign of him or his sausages was to be seen. Simon crawled under the bramble bush, but there was nothing there but dead leaves.

"Oh, Jill, whatever shall we do?" he said. "We can't take Pincher home like this. Nobody would believe he was Pincher, and he might easily be caught by a cat."

Jill began to cry. She did so love Pincher, and it was dreadful to think he was only a mouse now, not a jolly, romping puppy-dog.

"That must have been a gnome or a brownie," she said, wiping her eyes. "Well, Simon, I'm not going home with Pincher like that! Let's go farther into the wood and see if we meet any more little folk. If there's one here, there must be others. We'll ask them for help if we meet them."

So they went on down the little winding path. Simon carried Pincher in his pocket, for there was plenty of room there for the little dog, now that he was only a mouse!

After they had gone a long way they saw the oddest little house. It had two legs underneath it, and it stood with its back to the children. Simon caught hold of Jill's arm and pointed to it in amazement. They had never seen a house with legs before.

"Oh!" cried Jill, stopping in surprise. "It's got legs!"

The house gave a jump when it heard Jill's voice, and then, oh goodness me, it ran off! Yes, it really did! You should have seen its little legs twinkling as it scurried away between the trees. The children were too astonished to run after the house. They stood and stared.

"This is a funny part of Cuckoo Wood," said Simon. "Look! There are more of those houses with legs!"

Jill looked. Sure enough, in a little clearing stood about six more of the little houses. Each one had a pair of legs underneath, and shoes on their big feet.

Jill and Simon walked towards the funny houses – but dear me, as soon as they came near, the houses took to their heels and ran off as fast as ever they could! The children ran after them, but they couldn't run fast enough to catch them.

The children were just about to give up when they saw one of the houses stop. It moved on again, but it was limping badly.

"We could catch that one!" said Jill. "Come on!"

They ran on and in a few minutes they had caught up the limping house. Just as they got near it the door opened and a pixie looked out. She was very lovely, for her curly golden hair was as fine as spider's thread, and her wings shone like dragonfly wings.

"Oh, dear. What's the matter, little house?" the pixie asked. "Why are you limping?"

Then the pixie looked up and saw the children. She stared at them in surprise.

"Oh, so that's why the houses ran off!" she said. "They saw you coming! Could you help me, please, children? I think my house has a stone in one of its shoes, and I'm not strong enough to get it out all by myself."

Jill and Simon were only too ready to help. Simon held up one side of the house whilst the house put up one of its feet so that they could remove its big shoe. The pixie and Jill found a big stone in the shoe. They shook out the stone and replaced the shoe. The little house made a creaking noise that sounded just like "Thank you!"

"What a funny house you've got!" said Jill to the little pixie.

"What's funny about it?" asked the pixie in surprise, shaking back her long curly hair. "It's just the same as all my friends' houses."

"But it's got legs!" said Simon. "Where we come from, houses don't have legs at all. They just stand square on the ground and never move at all, once they are built."

"They sound silly sort of houses," said the pixie. "Suppose an enemy came? Why, your house couldn't run away! Mine's a much better house than yours."

"Oh, much better," agreed Jill. "I only wish I lived in a house like this. It would be lovely. You'd go to sleep at night and wake up in a different place in the morning, because the house might wander miles away."

"I say, pixie, I wonder if you could help us!" suddenly said Simon. He took the little mouse out of his pocket. "Look! This was our puppy-dog, Pincher, and a nasty little man changed him into a mouse. Could you change him back into a dog again, please?"

"Oh no," said the pixie. "You need very strong magic for that. I only know one person with that kind of magic, and that's High-Hat the Giant."

"Where does he live?" asked Jill eagerly.

"Miles away from here," said the pixie. "You have to go to the Rainbow's End, and then fly up to Cloud-Castle just half-way up the rainbow."

"Goodness, we couldn't possibly go there," said Jill. "We haven't wings like you, pixie."

"Well, Dumpy the gnome lives near the Rainbow's End," said the pixie. "He keeps pigs that fly, you know, so he might lend you two of them. But I don't know if High-Hat the Giant will help you, even if you go to him. If he's in a bad mood he won't do anything for anybody."

"Well, we must try," said Simon. "Which is the way to the Rainbow's End?"

"It depends where there's a rainbow today," said the pixie. "I know! I'll get my house to take you there. It always knows the way to anywhere. Come inside and we'll start. You helped me to get the stone out of my house's shoe, and I'd like to help you in return."

"But we're too big to fit into your little house,"
said Jill.

"Don't worry," laughed the pixie. "As soon as you
set foot on the doorstep, you'll shrink to fit!"

And so they did! As soon as Jill and Simon climbed
onto the step they became pixie-sized. It was all very
exciting.

The pixie shut the door, and told the children to sit down. It was a funny house inside, more like a carriage than a house, for a bench ran all around the wall. A table stood in the middle of the room and on it were some dishes and cups. In a corner a kettle boiled on a stove, and a big grandfather clock ticked in another corner.

The clock had two feet underneath it, like the house, and it gave the children quite a fright when it suddenly walked out from its corner, had a look at them and then walked back.

"Don't take any notice of it," said the pixie. "It hasn't any manners, that old clock. Would you like a cup of cocoa and some daffodil biscuits?"

"Oooh yes, please," said both the children at once. The pixie made a big jug of cocoa and put some funny yellow biscuits in the shape of a daffodil trumpet on a plate. They were delicious. The cocoa was lovely too, it tasted like chocolate and lemonade mixed together. The children did enjoy their funny meal.

Then the pixie spoke to her house. "Take us to the Rainbow's End," she said. "As quickly as you can."

To the children's great delight the house began to run. They felt as if they were on the sea, or on the elephant's back at the Zoo, for the house rocked from side to side as it scampered along. Jill looked out of the window.

"Simon, look! There are hundreds of fairy folk here!" cried Jill, in excitement. So there were – crowds of them, going about shopping, talking and wheeling funny prams with the dearest fairy babies inside.

The grandfather clock walked out of its corner to the window too, and trod on Jill's toe. It certainly had no manners, that clock.

They passed right through the town and went up a hill where little blue sheep were grazing. Looking after them was a little girl exactly like Bo-peep. The pixie said yes, it really was Bo-peep. That was where she lived. It was a most exciting journey, and the children were very sorry when they saw a great rainbow in the distance. They knew they were coming to the end of their journey.

The little house stopped at one end of the rainbow. The children stepped outside. The glittering rainbow towered above them. It was far wider than a road, and the colours were almost too bright to look at.

"Now High-Hat lives half-way up the rainbow," said the pixie, pointing. "Come along, I'll take you to Dumpy the gnome. He may have a couple of pigs to lend you."

She took them to a squat little house not far from the rainbow. Outside was a big yard, and in it were a

crowd of very clean, bright-pink pigs with pink wings on their backs.

"Hie, Dumpy, are you at home?" cried the pixie. The door of the house flew open and a fat gnome with twinkling eyes peeped out.

"Yes, I'm at home," he said. "What can I do for you?"

"These children want to fly to High-Hat's," said the pixie. "But they haven't wings. Could you lend them two of your pigs?"

"Yes, if they'll promise to be kind to them," said Dumpy. "The last time someone borrowed my pigs he whipped them and all the curl came out of their tails."

"Oh, these children are very kind. They helped me to take a stone out of my house's shoe," said the pixie. "You can trust them. Which pigs can they have, Dumpy?"

"This one and that one," said the fat little gnome. "Catch hold of their tails, children, and jump on. Hold on to their collars, and, what ever you do, speak kindly to them or the curl will come out of their tails."

Jill and Simon caught hold of the curly tails of the two pigs and jumped on. The pigs' backs were rather slippery, but they held on tight. Suddenly the fat little animals rose into the air, flapped their pink wings and flew up the shining rainbow. It was such a funny feeling. The pigs talked to one another in queer little squeals, and the children were careful to pat them kindly in case the curl came out of their tails.

In ten minutes they came to a towering castle. It was wreathed in clouds at the top, and was made of a strange black stone that reflected all the rainbow colours in a very lovely manner. It didn't *seem* a real castle, but it *felt* real enough when the children touched it. They jumped off the pigs backs and patted them gratefully.

"Stay here, dear little pigs, till we come out again," said Simon. Then he and Jill climbed the long flight of shining black steps to the castle door. Simon knocked loudly. The noise echoed through the sky like thunder.

"Come in!" called a deep voice from inside the castle. Simon pushed open the door and went in. He found himself in a great high room full of a pale silvery light that looked like moonlight. Sitting at a table, frowning hard, was a giant.

He was very, very big, so big that Jill wondered if he could possibly stand upright in the high room. He was sucking a pencil and looking crossly at a book in front of him.

"Good morning," said Simon politely.

"It isn't a good morning at all," snapped the giant. "It's a bad morning. I can't get these sums right again."

"Well, bad morning, then," said Jill. "We've come to ask your help."

"I'm not helping anyone today," growled the giant. "I tell you I can't get these sums right. Go away."

"We *must* get his help," whispered Simon to Jill.

"What sums are they?" Jill asked the giant. To their great surprise High-Hat suddenly picked them up in his great hand and set them by him on the table. When she had got over her fright Jill looked at the giant's book.

She nearly laughed out loud when she saw the sums that were puzzling the giant. This was one of them: "If two hens, four dogs and one giant went for a walk together, how many legs would you see?"

"I'll tell you the answer," she said. "It's twenty-two!"

The giant turned to the end of the book and looked at the answers.

"Yes!" he said in astonishment. "You're right! But how did you know that? Do another sum, please."

Jill did all the sums. They were very easy indeed. When they were all finished Simon thought it was time to ask for help again.

"Could you help us now?" he asked. "We've helped *you*, you know."

"I've told you, this is one of my *bad* mornings," said the giant crossly. "I *never* help people on a bad morning. Please go away, and shut the door after you."

Jill and Simon stared at him in despair. What a nasty giant he was, after all the help they had given him too! It really was too bad.

"I don't believe you know any magic at all!" said Jill. "Why, you couldn't even do easy sums!"

The giant frowned till the children could scarcely see his big saucer-like blue eyes. Then he jumped up in a rage and hit his head hard against the ceiling. He sat down again.

"I will punish you for saying a rude thing like that!" he thundered. "Listen! You can just sit there all year long and ask me to do one thing after another. I'll show you how powerful I am! And the first time you can't think of anything, I'll turn you into ladybirds!"

Goodness! Jill and Simon turned quite pale. But in a trice Simon took the little brown mouse out of his pocket and showed it to the giant.

"You couldn't possibly turn this mouse into a puppy-dog, I'm sure!" he cried.

The giant gave a snort and banged his hand on the table. "Homminy, tinkabooroyillabee, juteray, bong!" he cried. And hey presto, the little mouse grew bigger and bigger, and there was Pincher again, as large as life. But the giant left the children no time to think.

"Next thing, please!" he cried.

"Go to the moon and back!" cried Jill suddenly. In a trice High-Hat had vanished completely.

"Quick, he's gone to the moon!" cried Jill. "Come on, Simon, we'll escape before he comes back!"

Out of the castle door they ran, Pincher scampering after them. The two pigs were patiently waiting outside at the bottom of the castle steps. Jill and Simon jumped on their backs. Simon held Pincher safely in his arms as the flying pigs rose into the air and flew back to the end of the rainbow.

Just as they got there they heard a tremendous noise far up in the air.

"It's the giant, come back from the moon!" said Jill. "Goodness, what a noise he's making! It sounds like a thunderstorm."

The pixie came running to meet them.

"Is that High-Hat making all that noise?" she asked, looking frightened. "Give the pigs back to Dumpy, and climb into my house again with me. The next thing that

happens will be High-Hat sliding down the rainbow after you, and we'd better be gone before he arrives. He'll be in a dreadful temper!"

They gave the pigs back to the twinkling gnome, and thanked him. Then they climbed into the walking house.

Off they went at a great rate, far faster than before.

Pincher couldn't understand it. He began to bark and that annoyed the grandfather clock very much. It suddenly came out of its corner and boxed both Pincher's ears.

"I'm so sorry," said the pixie. "It's a very bad-mannered clock. I only keep it because it's been in my family for so many years. Oh, by the way, where do you want to go to?"

"Oh, home, please!" begged the children.

"Right!" said the pixie. Just as she said that there came the sound of a most tremendous BUMP, and the whole earth shook and shivered.

"There! The giant's slid down the rainbow!" said the pixie. "I knew he would bump himself."

The house went on and on. When it came to a sunshiny stretch of road it skipped as if it were happy.

"Here you are!" suddenly cried the pixie, opening her door. And sure enough, there they were. They were in their very own garden at home!

The children jumped out and turned to call Pincher, who was barking in excitement. Suddenly, the grandfather clock ran out of its corner and gave Pincher a smack as he ran out of the door.

"Oh dear, I'm so sorry!" cried the pixie. "It hasn't any manners at all, I'm afraid. Well, see you another day! Good-bye, good-bye!"

The little house ran off, and the children watched it go. What an adventure they had had had! And thank goodness they were back to their proper size and Pincher wasn't a mouse any longer, but a jolly, jumping puppy-dog.

"Come on, Pincher!" cried Simon. "Come and tell Mother all about your great adventure!"

Off they went and, dear me, Mother *was* surprised to hear their strange and exciting story!

The Very Old Teddy Bear

Barnaby, the teddy bear, was very old indeed. He belonged to a little boy called Billy. But he was older even than Billy, because once upon a time he had belonged to Billy's mother.

Billy's mother had loved her teddy bear very much, and she had never wanted to give him away. But when she had a little boy of her own, she brought old Barnaby out of the cupboard and gave him to Billy.

"There you are!" she said. "You can have old Barnaby, darling. He's so soft and cuddlesome. He's had to be sewn up here – and here – and his ears don't match now – but I expect you will love him because he looks so sweet."

Billy did love him. He took Barnaby to bed with him every night. He was such a very cuddly bear. You know, some toys are much more cuddly than others, and you feel as if you must cuddle up to them in bed. Well Barnaby was that kind of toy. Every night Billy would talk to the bear before he went to sleep and tell him all his secrets.

Billy played with Barnaby a lot when he was little. But as he got older, Billy began to play more and more with other toys. He particularly liked his new train engine and some clockwork cars his father had given him. He played with them all day. But he still took the old bear to bed with him every night.

On Billy's fifth birthday, he had a party and his friends came to play in the garden. All his friends had brought presents for him. Peter and Jane gave him a very neat sailor doll in a blue and white uniform. His cousin, Charles, gave him a clockwork dog that could run and wag its tail. He also had six toy soldiers in bright red and blue uniforms, a wind-up car, a football and a colouring book and crayons. After Billy had opened his presents the children went back outside to play.

While the children were playing in the
garden, the toys were getting to know one
another in the playroom. The new toys
were very proud of themselves
and they laughed
at old Barnaby.

"Whatever does Billy keep you for?"
they said. "A dirty, smelly old toy like you!
You look awful. Your ears don't match – and
did you know you have lost an eye?"

"Yes. I know," said the bear. "It fell down a crack in the floor. I couldn't get it out."

"You ought to be put in the dustbin," said the clockwork dog in disgust. "I don't like living in the same toy cupboard as you!"

"He won't be kept much longer," said the sailor doll. "Now we're here, Billy won't want him any more. Billy will throw him away – he's too old even to *give* away now!"

"Don't let's talk to him," said one of the soldiers. "Really, he's quite impossible!"

But the bear didn't seem to mind what they said. He smiled a little, and looked at them out of his one brown eye.

"You don't seem to mind the idea of being thrown away!" said the sailor doll, annoyed.

"I shan't be thrown away," said the bear.

"Well, you might be given away, or thrown into the back of the cupboard and never remembered again," said the clockwork dog.

"I shan't be forgotten, or given away," said Barnaby shaking his head. "I may fall to bits with old age – but I shan't be put into the dustbin – and I dare say I shall still be here when *you* are all broken and gone."

"What does he mean?" said the sailor doll to the toy soldiers. "He seems very sure about things. How does he know that he won't be thrown away?"

"He sits there and smiles, and he doesn't care a bit when we say these things to him," said one of the soldiers, puzzled.

"Dirty, ragged, smelly, ugly old thing!" said the clockwork dog. "I'd be afraid of the dustbin every minute of the day, if I was like him!"

But the old bear wasn't unhappy or worried. He just looked rather amused, as if he knew something that the others didn't know. They were so curious about it that at last they asked him.

"Why are you so sure that nothing horrid will happen to you?" asked the sailor doll at last. "Please tell us. You look as if you know something that we don't know."

"I do," replied Barnaby. "I know the biggest thing in the world, the only thing that can be trusted, and the most beautiful thing there is. And I know I am safe as long as it lasts."

"How are you safe? What do you know? What is the biggest thing in the world?" asked the other toys in surprise.

"Listen to me and I will tell you," said the teddy bear, looking at them out of his one brown eye.

"What do you see when you look at me? I know very well!" the old bear continued, smiling. "You see a dirty old bear, sewn up here and there because he got torn, with ears that don't match, and with only one eye, and no growl!"

He stopped. The others nodded. That was just what they did see.

"Well, Billy sees all that too, but it doesn't matter to him, because he loves me," said the old bear. "Love is the very biggest thing in the world, you know. I'm safe because Billy loves me."

"*He* won't put me into the dustbin, *he* won't give me away," Barnaby continued. "I'm Barnaby, the old bear he loves, the old bear his mother loved, the old bear that has snuggled up to him hundreds and hundreds of times!"

"Oh!" said the sailor doll. "He must love you a lot, Barnaby."

"He does," said Barnaby. "I'm a lucky bear, because I've been loved a lot. I've loved Billy's mother too, and of course I love Billy. No wonder I'm happy."

"Yes. No wonder you are happy," said the clockwork dog. "I'd like to be loved like that too. You must feel very safe when you are loved. It's a pity there isn't more love in the world, Barnaby. There doesn't seem enough to go round."

"There is really," said the old bear wisely, "but we don't all do our share, and love one another. I know you hate me, for instance – but I can't help being old and ragged."

"No – we don't hate you," said the sailor doll, looking suddenly ashamed. "We weren't very wise, that's all. We didn't think about this biggest thing in the world. Please be friends, will you?"

"Of course," said Barnaby, delighted. "I'll do anything I can for you – I'll tell you stories of the time when Billy's mother was a little girl, if you like. I know such a lot of stories."

But before he could tell them a story, Billy came in.

"Where's old Barnaby?" he said. "Oh, there you are. Come along, I want to cuddle you tonight, because I feel lonely now all my friends have gone. I know I'm five and a big boy, but I still need you. We'll snuggle up in bed together, dear old cuddly bear!"

"How Billy loves that old bear!" said the sailor doll to the others. "No wonder he feels safe. It must be nice to be loved like that. Let's be friendly and loving to him, now – shall we? He really is such a nice old bear."

"Why don't we have a party tomorrow to thank Barnaby for being so kind to us. It will show him that we really are sorry for being so nasty and unloving to him," said the clockwork dog, wagging his tail.

And that's exactly what they did. The next day all the toys had a lovely party and Barnaby was the guest of honour.

The toys had a lovely time playing games together. They soon became the best of friends and they never forgot the lesson that the old bear had taught them about loving one another.

That all happened quite a long time ago now, and I expect you wonder what has happened to old Barnaby.

Well, he belongs to Billy's little sister now, and she takes him to bed every night, and loves him. So he knows quite a lot about the biggest thing in the world, doesn't he – lucky old bear!

THE END